On the Trail of the Bushman

On the Trail of the Bushman

ANITA DAHER

ORCA BOOK PUBLISHERS

Library and Archives Canada Cataloguing in Publication

Daher, Anita, 1965-
On the trail of the bushman / written by Anita Daher.

(Orca young readers)
ISBN 978-1-55469-013-8

I. Title. II. Series: Orca young readers

PS8557.A35O5 2009 jC813'.6 C2009-900020-2

First published in the United States, 2009
Library of Congress Control Number: 2008943723

Summary: Junior Canadian Ranger Tommy Toner has a secret, and his guilt is eating away at him and putting his friends in danger.

Orca Book Publishers gratefully acknowledges the support for its publishing programs provided by the following agencies: the Government of Canada through the Book Publishing Industry Development Program and the Canada Council for the Arts, and the Province of British Columbia through the BC Arts Council and the Book Publishing Tax Credit.

Cover artwork by Glenn Bernabe
Author photo by Sara Daher

ORCA BOOK PUBLISHERS
PO Box 5626, STN. B
VICTORIA, BC CANADA
V8R 6S4

ORCA BOOK PUBLISHERS
PO Box 468
CUSTER, WA USA
98240-0468

www.orcabook.com
Printed and bound in Canada.
Printed on 100% PCW recycled paper.

12 11 10 09 • 4 3 2 1

For my mother and father, and their love of adventure,
which infected me like a virus—but a good one—driving me
to spend my life gorging whenever and wherever possible
on new sights, sounds, cultures and experiences.
Life is beautiful. I understand this because of them.

Chapter One

"Everyone get dressed and get out!" Captain Conrad spoke urgently as he flipped on the lights and woke the boys in Tommy Toner's bunkhouse. Outside, alarms were sounding and people were shouting. The smell of smoke was overpowering.

"Is the camp on fire, Captain Conrad?" Tommy asked, shaking off sleep.

"It's the cookhouse, but we're worried it might spread. Follow me, boys! We'll form a bucket brigade until the fire department gets here!"

Tommy was bunking with fifteen other Junior Canadian Rangers—JCRs for short—led by the Canadian Rangers. The Canadian Rangers were known as the "eyes and ears" of Canada's North. The JCRs were the organization's youth group. Tommy had arrived three days ago as one of 185 boys and girls from across the North lucky enough to attend the annual JCR summer camp in Whitehorse, Yukon Territory.

Right now Tommy didn't feel very lucky.

A flying pillow to his head knocked him back to his senses.

"Come on, Tommy!" his friend Colly shouted. "Get it together!"

"Right!" Tommy said with a quick smile. The situation was serious, but Tommy couldn't help smiling. He always smiled. He was the type of person who smiled because it was sunny or because he was out in his boat. Everyone knew that about him. He was just a happy Inuvialuit boy from the small northern community of Tuktoyaktuk on Canada's Arctic coast. But he was absolutely serious right now, despite the quick smile. It was just his way of saying "I hear you."

With heart pounding and blood racing, he quickly pulled on his clothes and followed Colly and the other boys out the door to a line of JCRs that stretched up from the river. Even though it was the middle of the night, there was still plenty of light. When the July sun did disappear in this part of the North, it wasn't for long. Tommy and his bunkmates joined the line close to the fire. Captain Conrad and other Rangers passed out water-soaked strips of cloth for the JCRs to wrap around their heads and faces. Then the Rangers took their places closest to the flames.

With Rangers shouting instructions down each line, water sloshed forward toward the cookhouse, which was completely engulfed in flames. Tommy's eyes burned from the smoke as he passed each bucket forward, but he made sure the wet cloth was well wrapped around his face.

"Captain Conrad!" Colly shouted from behind him, his voice slightly muffled by his makeshift bandana. "Look!"

Tommy looked where Colly was pointing. Next to the cookhouse, fire was licking up the roof of the games hut! The wind must have carried the flames from one building to the next. Tommy knew without being told that if they didn't work fast, the same thing could happen to all the other buildings in the camp!

"My team, form another line!" Captain Conrad shouted. Tommy heard another Ranger shout the same thing down the line. Now they had two lines of JCRs. They spaced themselves so that they were farther apart but could still pass the buckets. The only problem was that each line now had half as many buckets. "Captain Conrad, do we have more buckets?" Tommy shouted.

Captain Conrad was busy speaking with another Ranger and didn't hear. Or maybe the wet cloth muffled his voice. There was no time to wait.

"There are more buckets in the laundry hut," Tommy said to Colly. "I'll get them."

Colly nodded. "Good idea—be quick!"

The laundry hut was just past the horseshoe pits between the games hut and the sleeping cabins. It would only take him a moment.

Suddenly, there was a crash as part of the roof from the cookhouse caved in. Despite their efforts, the buckets of water hadn't helped. Not enough anyway. Maybe they'd started fighting it too late. But they could still try to save the games cabin and the rest of the camp.

Where was the fire department?

"Go!" Colly shouted, passing another bucket forward.

Tommy sprinted across the space between the buildings, pulled open the door to the laundry cabin and peered inside. Against the wall there were more buckets—at least five! He grabbed them by the handles and ran back outside, banging against the doorframe on his way through. The bang must have vibrated all the way up to the roof, as something loosened and wafted down in front of him. Burning tar paper! He glanced up. Oh no!

"Captain Conraaaad!" he shouted, buckets bouncing against his legs as he ran. "The laundry hut is on fire too!"

As the JCRs shifted lines again, giving up on the cookhouse, they could hear the sirens of approaching fire engines. Finally! Two tanker trucks and an ambulance pulled into the yard, and, faster than Tommy could blink, hoses were stretched and water arched toward the burning roofs and buildings.

The JCRs watched, standing well out of the way.

After the flames were doused, some of the firefighters continued to spray the outsides of the buildings, while others made their way inside. The JCRs shed their breathing cloths and relaxed. A few wandered over to chat with the ambulance attendants. Fortunately nobody looked hurt, although everyone was coughing and their eyes stung. "You did good work, JCRs," Captain Conrad told their group. His eyes looked tired and bloodshot. "I'm very proud of you."

"Too bad the kitchen is toast," Evan mumbled. He glanced at Tommy. "No joke intended, okay?"

Evan was a JCR from Carcross, a town south of Whitehorse, close to the border of British Columbia. He was tall, with thick yellow hair that sprang from his head like the top of a dandelion, and he was always laughing at his own jokes and puns. To Tommy he looked like a giant Claymation character, but there was nothing animated about him right now. Like the rest of the JCRs, Evan looked tired, and soot streaked his face. Tommy nodded and smiled at Evan. This time his smile meant, "I understand."

Even with the fire out, there was no way anyone would be going back to sleep. Besides, the wash of light behind the dark sky signaled the approach of dawn.

Tommy looked across the yard and saw his friend Jaz. Tommy had met her and Colly when they had visited Tuktoyaktuk earlier that summer. The three of them had caught some gyrfalcon poachers and had kidded each other that they were northern superheroes.

But even superheroes couldn't do much against a raging fire.

Jaz waved and smiled. Her smile always meant only one thing: "I'm ready for anything!"

Movement near Tommy's group caught his attention, and he turned. One of the firefighters had joined Captain Conrad and some of the other Rangers. His yellow and silver coat was charred, and his gloves were completely black. He pushed his helmet back from the top of his head and wiped his forehead, leaving a black streak across it. The JCRs gathered close to hear what he was saying.

"What's the word, Chief?" Captain Conrad asked.

"That first building is gone, but I think you knew that. The second has significant damage to the roof, but you should be able to save it. The third we caught in time. Damage was minimal."

"Any idea what started it?" Colly asked. Tommy looked at his friend, standing straight and tall, eyes narrowed and intense. Colly was a Déné with blue eyes, which was unusual for an Aboriginal boy, but not unusual in Colly's family. When he was younger he'd been teased quite a lot. Tommy figured that was why he was usually so serious about everything.

"Hard to say for sure until we complete our investigation," the fire chief said. "But we found the hotspot in the muskeg behind that first building. And," he said, pulling out a small shiny object, "we found this. Might be what started it."

Tommy's stomach dropped along with his smile.

It couldn't be...could it?

Was the fire his fault?

Chapter Two

The fire chief held up a grape-soda can, partially flattened. It was the one Tommy had used. He was sure of it.

"How can that start a fire?" he asked in a small voice.

"The sun has been pretty hot over this past week," the fire chief said. "The bottom of this pop can could have acted like a parabolic mirror. You know what that is?" When Tommy nodded, the fire chief continued. "Could be that the sun bounced off it and set the muskeg smoldering. A regular mirror couldn't do it, but something like this, dish-shaped to focus the beam of light and polished up, it's a fire starter."

"You think someone did it on purpose?" Captain Conrad asked.

The fire chief shrugged. "We won't know for sure until we finish our investigation."

A rushing in Tommy's ears blocked out whatever Captain Conrad and the chief said next. All he could think about was how he'd been drinking a grape soda in the games room while listening to the others tell scary stories. He'd been trying hard to think up a really good story, one that would make his friends' eyes bug out. While he was thinking, he'd twisted the soda can around and around on his knee, polishing the bottom.

He'd been glad that lunchtime had arrived before it was his turn, because he hadn't come up with anything. The window in the games room was open, so he'd crushed the can against his knee and tossed it outside toward the garbage bin. Instead of landing inside, it had bounced and sailed off somewhere on the other side. Tommy hadn't wanted to go searching for it right then. If he'd done that, he would have been late for lunch! He promised himself that he would pick it up later.

Except he forgot.

It must have landed near the cookhouse. And it must have started the fire.

"...in any case," the fire chief was saying to Captain Conrad, "we should know soon if the fire was deliberately set."

"If it was, it wasn't by anyone here, Chief," Captain Conrad said. "These are all good kids, and they know the dangers of fire, especially this time of year when conditions are so hot and dry. They wouldn't be so foolish."

"Well, I know the owner hires a couple of homeless folks to clean the place up between camps. He lets them stay here for a while and makes sure they're well fed. Maybe one of those folks left the can out there. If our investigation determines the fire was deliberately set, we'll find them and question them."

Tommy gulped. The fire hadn't been started by a homeless person. It had been him. "But it's just a can. It must have been an accident!"

"You're probably right," the chief said, "but we have to check everything."

Tommy felt sick. He wanted to do the right thing... to speak up and say the soda can was his. But he couldn't. He opened his mouth to say something, but nothing came out. He thought about how they'd been warned by their leaders to be on their best behavior.

Usually the JCRs borrowed the cadet facilities for their summer camp. This year, however, the cadet camp was already being used, so they were at a private camp. They were supposed to take care of it. *Good* care! Instead, Tommy's stupidity and carelessness had destroyed one building and damaged two others.

If he confessed, they would never be allowed back.

And once the cadets heard about what happened, no way would the JCRs be welcome in their camp either! That would be awful beyond imagining. Not only for the 185 JCRs who were chosen to attend this year, but for all 350 of them across the North. He closed his mouth and swallowed his words. He was not smiling. Not on the outside, and not on the inside either.

Despite his misery, his stomach growled. As if he'd heard, Evan spoke up. "What will we do about breakfast, Captain Conrad?"

Captain Conrad looked at his watch. "I guess it is pretty close to mealtime, isn't it?" he said. "Let me check with the others, but I expect we can fire up some barbecues and have a cookout on the beach. Most of our supplies were safe in the cache." Captain Conrad gestured to the platform that had been built between four tall lodgepole-pine trunks, all stripped of their branches. The cache was used to keep food and supplies safe from bears and other animals.

They washed, returned to their bunkhouses and pulled on their green Junior Canadian Ranger sweatshirts and ballcaps, just like any other morning. This morning, however, as they gathered again on the beach and divvied up breakfast-making tasks, there was none of the usual fooling around.

The Rangers shut themselves in one of the buildings to discuss the fire and what would happen next, while the JCRs ate pancakes and bacon prepared on the barbecues. To Tommy, the food might as well have been soggy cardboard. He knew that he should tell Captain Conrad about the soda can. He had to! It was wrong not to admit the fire was his fault. Swallowing a big ball of buzzing nerves, he willed himself to stand and began moving toward the cabin.

"Where are you going?" Jaz asked.

Before he could answer, the door to the cabin banged open. Captain Conrad was first out, followed by Major Chris, who was in charge of all the JCRs across the North. They were followed by the other Rangers, all wearing their red Ranger sweatshirts and ballcaps.

Tommy stepped back. Major Chris raised a bull-horn to his mouth and spoke. "Is this thing on?" he asked. When there was no response, he tapped it to his leg and then put it up to his eye as if it were a telescope, before putting it back to his mouth. "If you cannot hear me, this thing is no good for talking. Maybe I should make it into a plant holder?"

Tommy heard snickering. He didn't join in.

"Ah, good!" Major Chris said. "It is working! In that case, I have something very important to tell you."

Tommy felt his breakfast turn to clay in the bottom of his belly.

"What happened last night was a terrible thing, but I want you to know that camp will carry on!"

The response from the JCRs was happy but subdued, as if they didn't want to sound *too* happy, given what had happened.

"What? This does not matter to you?" Major Chris asked.

"Yes, it matters!" Jaz piped up, close to the front.

"Ah, good," Major Chris said. "To Jaz it matters. Does it matter to anyone else?"

"Yes, sir!" came a collective shout.

"I can't hear you," Major Chris said.

"Yes, sir!" The shout came again, louder this time.

"Good!" Major Chris said. "Our plans will change a little bit this week, as we work together to rebuild the destroyed building, but I want you to know that together we can do this. You are Junior Canadian Rangers. When there is trouble in your community, you are always first to help. Your Ranger leaders and I are going to be organizing the rebuilding today, so our planned activities have changed. But we have something fun for you to do while we're busy."

"What?" Jaz called. "Are we going to dress up like in old Klondike days and put on a play?"

Major Chris stared at her for a moment and then burst out laughing. After a moment he wiped his eyes. "No, Jaz, but that is a very good idea. Maybe we'll do that another time." He stepped back and motioned for Captain Conrad to take the bullhorn.

"As you know," Captain Conrad said, "the Yukon is full of legends, mysteries and incredible true tales of heroism. Today you will spend time in Whitehorse at the library and museum, and you will go on walking tours. You will read and listen and find a story you want to tell about the Yukon. Tonight we will share these stories around our campfires."

"When will we fix the cookhouse?" Jaz asked.

"We will begin working on it tomorrow," Captain Conrad said. "We will divide into cleaning crews and work in shifts. In the morning some of you will kayak, rappel and go horseback riding, just as we planned, and others will work on repairing and cleaning the camp. After lunch we will switch."

Tommy took a deep breath and let it out again as the JCRs cheered. He was relieved they weren't upset about the change in plans and that they would be able to repair the damage to the camp. Still, a part of him wished he could just melt away into the forest.

Chapter Three

After the breakfast cleanup was complete and bag lunches were prepared, the JCRs gathered in the parking lot and loaded into buses that would drop them downtown for the day. Tommy sat silently with Colly, which seemed to suit Colly just fine. Colly was quiet by nature and often rolled his eyes at Jaz's chattering. Jaz and Evan sat in the seat just ahead of them, joking and laughing as if the fire hadn't even happened.

The bus driver was in a good mood as well. As he toured them around Whitehorse, he not only pointed out sights, but he also sang about them! His songs didn't make much sense or even rhyme very well, but he didn't seem to care. Neither did anyone else. They even tried to join in.

"Hey, mister bus driver, what's that over there?" one girl sang out.

"Why that, young miss, is not just a house and a tree; it's the actual residence of Sam McGee!"

Everyone knew who Sam McGee was. Last night after supper, they'd learned about the famous poet, Robert Service, who had lived in Whitehorse during the Klondike Gold Rush more than a hundred years ago. Captain Conrad had recited one of Robert Service's most famous poems, *The Cremation of Sam McGee.*

The bus driver sang that Sam McGee wasn't really from Tennessee like the poem said, but from somewhere in Ontario.

The songs came to an end at the museum, and the JCRs tumbled out, meeting up with friends who were getting out of other buses. Tommy could hear snatches of melody and guessed they were keeping up the fun and talking—or rather, singing—about their driver.

The McBride Museum was a collection of buildings. The first one housed the gift shop and all the main displays, and there were smaller buildings out the side doors. One of them was a log cabin with moose antlers above the door and a sign indicating that it was Sam McGee's cabin. The guy was everywhere!

Tommy watched Colly peer at the cards in front of the critter room, while Jaz disappeared downstairs into something called the "Clutteratorium." He wandered into the yard where Evan and some of the others were getting ready to try their hands at gold panning.

Evan held up his pan for Tommy to see. "Hey, Tommy, do you know the difference between pea soup and roast beef?"

"Uh...what?"

"Everybody knows how to roast beef."

He must have looked confused, because Jaz, who had just bounced up beside him, burst out laughing, "Pea soup, Tommy? Don't you get it? Everyone knows how to *roast* beef, but how do you *pee* soup?"

Tommy sighed. "Yeah, I get it Jaz."

As Jaz and Evan sloshed pans of water and sand, looking for tiny flecks of gold, he turned Evan's joke over in his head. What exactly did pea soup have to do with panning for gold? It was probably just an excuse to tell a groaner of a joke.

"Hey, Jaz," Evan said, "what color is a burp?"

"I know that one! It's *burple*," she said as she erupted in giggles.

He left them to their gold and their dumb jokes.

Inside one building, Colly was engrossed in studying old photos and only grunted when Tommy said hello. Shrugging, Tommy moved off, making his way through groups of fellow JCRs. Some of them didn't appear to be looking very hard for stories. One display was an old North West Mounted Police jail cell, and JCRs were taking turns "locking" themselves in and then confessing their crimes.

"I admit I ate the last piece of lemon pie!" someone cried out.

Tommy knew that if he had the guts to confess his crime, it would blow their socks off. He sniffed. The smell of the fire clung to them, despite their washup before breakfast. Tommy didn't think any amount of soap would remove the scent from his skin.

Being a Junior Canadian Ranger wasn't all about hunting, camping and having fun. Like Major Chris had said: When there was trouble in a community, JCRs were always first to help. Being a JCR was also about *honor*. Keeping quiet about starting the fire—even if it *was* an accident—wasn't very honorable.

It was pretty much the same as telling a lie. Letting everyone think a homeless person had started it was downright shameful.

He moved past the jail without stopping.

After they finished with the museum, the JCRs visited the offices of the *Whitehorse Star* newspaper and listened to the editor tell stories about some of the colorful people who came to the Yukon during the Klondike Gold Rush in 1897. After that they had a chance to tour Sam McGee's old house—the one the bus driver had sung about. Now it was a bed and breakfast, and the owner, Bernie, told them about the ghosts that had been seen there.

"Wouldn't the ghosts make people scared to sleep?" Shelby asked. Shelby was a JCR from Colly's and Jaz's home community of Destiny. Like Colly, she was Déné, but her eyes were the color of a polished penny.

"The sightings are never sinister," Bernie assured them. "Sometimes it even seems like they want to help."

"How?" Shelby asked.

"Well…one woman woke to a ghost nurse sitting on her bed, telling her everything would be okay."

As they left the B and B, the JCRs were told they had free time over lunch and were to meet their buses on Main Street in an hour. Tommy walked alone beside the river, ate a screaming-hot burrito from a truck in the park and then cooled his mouth with a tiger-tiger ice-cream cone from a fifties-style diner on Main Street.

Two tables over, a man and a woman sat in a booth. They were leaning so close together their foreheads almost touched. Tommy could hear their loud whispers.

"I don't care what the experts say," the man said. "Auntie smelled burnt hair, and you know what that means!"

The woman nodded. "Yes, and something has been raiding your traplines."

Tommy tried not to listen, but he couldn't help it.

"Come on, JCRs, it's time to go!" he heard from the open door to the street. He zipped his jacket and climbed aboard his bus, once again finding a seat close to Colly and Jaz.

Colly was looking at him and frowning. Tommy could feel his face flush.

"What are you staring at, man?" he asked.

"Nothing," Colly said. "I was just wondering if you're feeling okay."

"I'm fine." He wondered if his guilt was so obvious that it made him look different.

After supper several campfires were lit, and the JCRs broke into groups to share stories.

In Tommy's group, Shelby told the story of Kate Carmack, whose real name was Shaaw Tlaa. She was from the Tagish First Nation, but she married her dead sister's husband after her own husband and daughter died. His name was George Carmack. George, along with Kate's brother, Skookum Jim, and her cousin, Dawson Charlie, had staked the claims that started the Klondike Gold Rush.

Colly had read a ten-year-old news story about a man who killed his wife's best friend and took off into the bush, never to be seen again.

"Why did he kill her?" Tommy asked.

"All it says was that they had a fight. It was a big mystery where he went. Some people thought he probably went to Mexico, and other people thought he ended up in the bush somewhere, or maybe dead."

Jaz told the story of a wolf that made friends with a family while they were at their summer camp.

Evan nodded. "I heard that can happen. Say, what do you call a lost wolf?"

"What?" the JCRs said together.

"A *where* wolf!"

They all groaned.

"How about you, Tommy? Did you find any stories?" Evan asked.

He thought for a minute and then he nodded. "Yeah, but not at the museum. I heard something while I was eating ice cream at the diner. There was a man and a woman talking about a bushman that scared their auntie not too far from here."

"What's a bushman?" Jaz asked.

"Sasquatch," Shelby said. "Or sometimes they call it Bigfoot."

Evan leaned into the circle. "Some people think a sasquatch is the same as a windigo!"

"Actually, the bushman has many names, depending on where you are," Shelby said. "The Salish people in British Columbia call it Boq."

"How do you know all this?" Colly asked, looking impressed.

"I did a project for school," Shelby said. "Plus, my grandmother told me stories."

Evan stood and gave a bloodcurdling shriek, which silenced JCR groups all down the beach. "That's what a windigo sounds like," he explained. "You don't ever want to hear one outside your camp, believe me!"

Tommy shivered.

"So what happened to the bushman those people were talking about today?" Colly asked Tommy. "Did they go after him?"

"They said a tuft of fur it left behind was tested in Alberta, but it ended up being from a bear."

"Oh," the others said. They shrugged and turned away, as if disappointed.

It didn't matter. Tommy hadn't been much in the mood to tell stories anyway.

Chapter Four

The next morning, the JCRs divided into work and activity groups. Tommy was in one of six groups that would spend the morning horseback riding on old prospector trails.

"Good morning, JCRs!" their trail leader, Jodi, called out. Jodi was the owner of Emerald Lake Ranch and Horseback Adventures. In a long oilskin ranch coat and a cowboy hat, she looked like she had just stepped out of the Old West. She was leading two horses. Several ranch hands, each of them leading two horses, milled around with the JCRs. "Here are your mounts," Jodi announced. "Say hello!"

They'd been allowed to choose their own trail groups. Shelby suggested that she, Tommy, Colly, Jaz and Evan should ride together, seeing as they'd all gotten along so well at the campfire the night before. Tommy wondered whether Evan would tell jokes the whole way. That would be better than screaming like a windigo.

Tommy was relieved to be away from the camp for a while. Away from the reminder of the terrible damage he had caused.

As Jodi and her ranch hands matched up riders and horses, Tommy breathed deeply. The smell of pine trees and warm horse was comforting, even though it was new to him. Tuktoyaktuk wasn't a place for horses.

With a smile, Jodi handed Tommy the reins of a stocky, light brown horse with a thin white blaze down its nose. Tommy stared at the beast as it blinked its big brown eyes at him. It looked like it expected him to do something. But what? After a moment it yawned.

"Before we head out for our ride," Jodi announced, "we need to go over a few basics."

When each group was matched with a trail leader, the JCRs learned how to sit, go, stop, and ride up and down hills. As the others began leading their horses around, getting to know them, Tommy stood still, reins clenched in his hands.

"You're Tommy, right?" Jodi asked.

Tommy nodded.

"Are you nervous about riding, Tommy?"

Tommy flushed. "No! It's just that...I don't know. It's just a bit weird."

Jodi grinned. "No sweat, Tommy. We've had lots of JCRs come here who'd never ridden a horse before. Would it help to know how a horse thinks?"

"Sure," Tommy said. "Maybe."

"In the wild, horses are prey animals, and even the best-trained ones never lose that instinct to get away from danger and discomfort."

"Does that mean it might take off on me?"

"My horses have seen pretty much everything in these woods, so they're not likely to get frightened. Horses are gentle, and they want to please. They also always try and move away from pressure, whether it's a threat from a wild animal in the bush, or a poke on the flank, like this."

As Tommy watched, she touched the right side of the horse's rear end and waited as it moved a step to the left. Then she moved around to the left and poked there. The horse stepped to the right.

"To turn, in addition to holding the reins like I've already shown you, if you press with your right knee or foot, the horse will move to the left. And if you press with your left knee or foot..." She looked at him, waiting for him to finish.

"It'll move right—away from the pressure."

"Yes! A horse wants to please, and it wants to keep things easy. Does that help?"

"I guess," he said.

"Ride with your whole body, Tommy, not just your hands, and you'll have a better time of it."

With a sigh, he looked at his horse. He stroked its toffee-colored neck and ran his palm along the smooth worn leather of the saddle. Jodi smiled her encouragement as he swung himself up into the saddle.

Oh, man!

He looked at the ground, feeling really tall, kind of wobbly and very weird.

The horse obviously didn't think it was any big deal. Jodi adjusted the stirrups to the right length and handed him the reins. "Here," she said. "Practice what I showed you while I get the others set up."

"Wait," Tommy called as Jodi turned to leave. "What's his name?"

Jodi smiled. "*Her* name is Timber. Don't worry, Tommy. She'll take good care of you."

He sat, unsure what to try first. After a moment, he felt Timber take a deep breath and let it out in a sigh. "What's the matter, Timber," he murmured, "are you bored?"

Tentatively, he clucked the way Jodi had shown them and gave Timber a nudge with both his feet. Timber's ears waggled back and forth, and she began walking forward. He felt a butterfly in his belly, but it wasn't because he was nervous. He pressed his right knee into her, and she turned to the left. This was pretty cool! He walked in circles with Timber while the others had their stirrups adjusted. He stopped and started and stroked his horse's neck. It was warm and soft.

Other groups melted into the woods in different directions, and soon Tommy's group was ready to go as well. They started up the trail with Jodi in the lead, followed by Jaz, Shelby, Tommy, Evan and Colly. He didn't feel shy about not having any horse experience, because he knew his friends were in the same boat. Well, maybe not Evan. After all, he lived not too far south of here. Tommy got the impression from Jodi that the Yukon was horse country, so Evan probably knew how to ride.

From the front of the line, Jodi was pointing out the landmarks surrounding the valley they were riding through: the snow-capped Caribou Mountain, Montana Mountain and Grey Ridge. At the top of a hill they paused. Below them was the most beautiful green-blue lake, ringed with white sand. "That's Emerald Lake," she said. "You can see why I named my ranch after it."

They continued along the trail, up and down hills, stopping once while Jodi pointed out the track of a grizzly bear. It must have been pretty fresh, because her horse danced around it and obviously wanted to get away. The other horses didn't seem to care and plodded along behind.

"Hey, what if that wasn't a bear track?" Jaz called over her shoulder.

"What are you talking about, Jaz?" Colly said.

"Maybe it was a bushman track. Tommy heard those people talking about it, remember?"

"Was it a bushman, or was it a windigo?" Evan asked.

"Bushman, I think," Tommy said. "What's the difference?" He knew that many communities had stories of the creatures, but not his. He guessed this was because it was a forest creature, and there were no forests in Tuktoyaktuk.

"The bushman is scary," Evan said, "but the windigo is terrifying. It can drive a person crazy with fear."

Shelby nodded. "My grandmother says it is unholy. It is a spirit that eats human flesh and can never, ever get enough."

Tommy shivered. "An evil spirit!" he said. "Why do people get them mixed up?"

"They are both spirits of some sort," Evan said. "A few years ago a hunter in BC saw some bushmen. He was with his family in a boat. It was night, but he could still see the creatures running back and forth along the shore."

"Good thing he was in a boat," Jaz said.

"Yes, but he was still scared," Evan said, "especially when the water started draining away. The bushmen made it happen. That's when he realized they were supernatural or something."

"So what about the windigo?" Jaz asked, halting her horse. The other JCRs stopped too.

"People don't like to talk about the windigo," Shelby said. "Some people say they are created when someone is cursed by a shaman or medicine person, or if they are bitten by a windigo or even just hear one pass close by. My grandma says that long ago, during times of famine, if someone got so hungry that they ate another person, they were possessed by the windigo spirit. They had to leave the community because they were afraid that the craving for human flesh would never leave them."

"Which is why you never want to hear a windigo scream outside your camp," Evan said.

Up ahead, Jodi kept going, humming to herself, like she didn't realize they'd stopped. Jaz turned in her saddle. "People must get them mixed up for a reason," she said. "Are windigos big and hairy, like bushmen?"

"Some people think so," Shelby said. "Others say windigos take on a monster form of the creatures they eat. So maybe if they eat wolves, they become werewolves. And if they eat people..."

Tommy felt the hairs on the back of his neck stand on end. "Maybe we should talk about something else," he said.

He could see Jaz grinning at him. "Are you afraid of werewolves, Tommy?"

They all turned and looked at him. He rolled his eyes and shook his head as if to say, "This is just crazy talk!" He wasn't afraid, not exactly, but didn't think it was a good idea to talk about things they didn't really understand. Before he could say anything, Evan's horse let out a loud honking sound from its back end. The JCRs began giggling.

"Hey, you guys!" They heard Jodi calling from somewhere ahead of them. "Make like squashed tomatoes, and *ketchup*!"

"Hey, I like that one!" Evan said as they each nudged their horses back up the path.

Tommy groaned with the others. He was glad to be on this soft sandy trail. With the forest canopy closing over their heads, he could almost forget the fire back at camp. Nothing seemed to matter more than this perfect moment, riding sweaty, farty horses in the mountains with his friends.

Chapter Five

With their horses tied to an old fence rail, they stopped for a rest in a clearing next to a river.

"Take a look here, kids," Jodi said, placing both hands on what looked like an old fencepost. "This is an actual stake that a gold miner drove into the riverbank, once upon a time."

"It looks really old," Shelby said.

"Maybe more than one hundred years old," Jodi said. "It could very well be from the Klondike Gold Rush."

"Hey, feel my forehead," Evan said. "I don't feel very good."

Jodi frowned. "What's wrong, Evan?"

"I think I have gold fever!"

Jodi grinned as the others groaned.

Tommy reached high above his head, stretching. It felt weird to walk after sitting on a horse for the past hour, like he might fall over at any moment. He shook his legs out as he wandered around the clearing. In the distance, poking up from behind pine trees, he could see a rounded bit of mountain. He called to the others. "That cliff over there looks like someone's head!"

"They call that the Crank," Jodi said.

"Is that because it looks like a cranky old man's head?" Jaz asked.

Jodi shrugged and smiled. "Maybe. It used to be a place to hike or ride if you wanted a good workout. The climb to the top is pretty steep."

"Used to?" Shelby asked. "What's wrong with it now?"

"I don't know. People just stopped going." She frowned. "There were rumors..."

"What kind of rumors?" Colly asked.

"Nothing specific. A few people said they got the creeps, like someone was watching them. After a while, it just sort of fell off the radar as a place to go."

"We should go!" Jaz cried.

Jodi chuckled. "I like your enthusiasm, girl, but I have another trail planned for us. We're going to follow this river to an old prospector's cabin."

"Will we see a real gold mine, Jodi?" Jaz asked. "Can we pan for gold?"

"There is an active gold mine in the area," Jodi said. "But it's a bit of a hike, even on horseback, and they haven't said they're up for visitors. So, no. Sorry, kiddo."

Jaz looked disappointed but only for a moment. She sidled up next to Tommy and whispered, "The Crank looks like much more of an adventure than looking at some musty old cabin. I've seen plenty of those!"

She started to bounce away but then stopped and looked back at him. "Is something wrong, Tommy?"

"No. Why?"

Jaz crinkled her brow. "I don't know. You just seem different from when Colly and I saw you in Tuk. You're not smiling as much."

"Maybe it's all these trees. I'm not used to them."

"Okay," she said, trotting back to where she'd left her horse.

“Hurry up, Tommy,” Jodi called. “Time to hit the trail!”

Tommy settled into the rhythm of the ride, hearing music in the creaking of leather saddles, the breathing of his horse, the wind, the twittering of birds and a squawk that reminded him of a squeaky screen door swinging open and closed.

“What kind of bird is that?” he asked Jodi.

“It’s a Steller’s jay,” she said, “a cousin of the blue jay. It moved up here from the south a few years ago. Brought a bunch of its buddies like some sort of an invasion! Keep your eyes peeled and you might see one hunting for seeds and nuts, or maybe a few bugs and frogs. It’s blue and black. Darker than the blue jay.”

“I’ve never seen any kind of a jay.”

“Oh, right,” Jodi said. “You’ll have other kinds of birds and animals up on the Arctic coast.”

“I think it’s cool how all the parts of the North are so different,” Jaz said.

The JCRs continued to chatter happily, but Tommy tuned them out. Instead he scanned the trees, hoping to see a Steller’s jay or another animal. Once he thought he saw a flash of blue, but figured his mind must be playing tricks on him, since it was ten times bigger than any other bird he'd seen in the forest.

"All right then," Jodi was saying. "If that is where you really want to go, we've got plenty of time, and I want you kids to have a ride you'll remember your whole lives!"

He gave his head a shake, suddenly realizing that some sort of decision-making had been going on while he was daydreaming. He felt annoyed that he had missed it. "What's happening?" he asked.

"Jaz here insists that when we broke for lunch she saw some sort of animal up on the Crank, and she wants to take a look. From here it's only about a ten-minute ride to the base of it. If you're all up for it, let's go!"

"I thought you said no one goes up there anymore."

Jodi tipped up the brim of her cowboy hat and rubbed her brow. "Yeah...but there's really no reason for that. From what I remember, it's got a good trail and gorgeous views at the top. Until we started talking about it, I hadn't thought of it in years."

Jaz bounced in her saddle. "Yay! We going up the Crank!" Her horse flicked its ears back and forth and showed the whites of its eyes. Tommy guessed it had never had to carry anyone quite like Jaz before.

They started off in single file, but Jaz hung back long enough to lean close to Tommy. "It wasn't exactly an animal I saw," she whispered.

"No? What was it?"

"I think it was a bushman!"

Something inside Tommy froze. "Are you kidding me?"

"I only saw it for a second. I guess it could have been a bear, but it looked like it was walking on two feet."

"Still could have been a bear."

"Nope. A bear would only walk like that for a minute. Whatever I saw kept walking." She clucked to her horse and sidled into the line just ahead of Tommy.

Tommy turned what Jaz said over and over in his mind. Jaz was the kind of person who always said a thing as soon as she thought it. Surely she hadn't *really* seen a bushman. If she had, she would have announced it to everyone.

He shrugged it off.

Before long, Jodi led them off the main path, deeper into the woods and onto a much narrower trail. The trees crowded them so tightly they had to stay in single file. Underneath the horses' hooves, the trail was stony. When Tommy's horse stumbled, he soothed her, stroking her neck. He didn't like the feeling of the forest crowding him. Finally, they climbed out of the dense brush to a more open area where he felt like he could breathe again. It was spooky though: birch-bark trees stripped bare of leaves, their branches turned gray and reaching like skeletal arms. "What happened here?" he asked Jodi.

"Could have been flooding. Too much water running off the mountain, maybe."

They were at the base of the Crank's "head." Here the trail began to get steep, as Jodi had promised, so they leaned forward in their saddles to make it easier on their horses. After a few minutes of climbing there was a flat stretch, and then the trail rose again.

"What's that sound?" Jaz asked.

Everyone stopped on the trail to listen to the rumbling. Tommy thought he could feel a vibration up through his saddle. After a minute it stopped.

"Sounds like it could have been a rock slide," Jodi said.

"Where?" Shelby asked. "Here on the Crank?"

"Maybe," Jodi said. "We won't know for sure unless we come to it. Small slides in this area aren't unusual."

Colly frowned. "That doesn't sound very safe," he said.

Jodi grinned. "Relax! It didn't sound close. Besides, as I recall, the trail isn't in a slide area." She waved them on. "Let's go!"

Up the trail they went, leaning into the steep bits. This time Jaz was in the lead, followed by Evan, Shelby, Colly and Tommy. Evan's horse started bugle-farting in earnest every time they went up a steep stretch. Tommy's horse began groaning, either because of the effort, or because she didn't appreciate what was coming out of Evan's horse's rear end.

"Hold up!" he heard Jodi cry from up front, and they all came to a stop. "Trail is blocked," she said. "Looks fresh—guess that rock slide was closer than it sounded."

"Guess this trail wasn't so safe after all," Colly muttered.

Tommy began maneuvering his horse out of the way so Jodi could get past him and lead them back the way they'd come. Another sudden vibration stopped him. "Uh-oh."

Shelby looked concerned. "What is it...oh!"

This time it was stronger. By the way they were looking around, reining in their horses, Tommy guessed that the others felt it as well. This time the rumbling sounded very close and it was getting louder! The horses flicked their ears back and forth. Jodi's horse danced around, clearly unhappy. The JCRs glanced about as if they expected rocks to fall on their heads, but none did. Almost as quickly as it began, it was over. Tommy released his grip on the saddle horn. His knuckles were white. He hadn't realized he'd been holding on so hard.

"Where are the rocks?" Shelby asked Jodi. She sounded out of breath, as if she'd been running.

Jodi didn't answer as she dismounted, moving toward the source of the sound. Tommy watched as she checked the path they'd just come from. It was the way back down to the bottom of the Crank. There was a deep frown line between Jodi's brows as she disappeared down the path. Hearing her curse, the JCRs glanced at each other.

Evan cleared his throat. "Why did the chicken cross the playground?" he asked.

"Um...I don't know," Tommy said. "Why?"

"To get to the other *slide*."

Nobody laughed.

Chapter Six

"Well, kids," Jodi said when she came back a few minutes later. "This is where we get creative."

"Are we trapped?" Tommy asked. He must have sounded peeved, because Colly gave him a sharp look. He didn't mean to sound that way, even though it was how he felt. If they'd gone to the prospector's cabin like they were supposed to, they wouldn't be in this jam!

He gave his head a shake. He'd been in tense situations before and had never been short-tempered about it. He guessed he was in a bad mood because of the fire. He gave his head another shake. He didn't want to think about it.

Jodi raised an eyebrow at him. "There are plenty of ways down a mountain, Tommy. We'll just find a new one." She dismounted. "Or at least a new way to connect with the old one. Everyone off," she said. "It's going to be pretty tight in some places. We'll lead our horses for a bit so we can better see where we're stepping."

Jodi did her best to find a way that wasn't too overgrown and was safe for them to walk.

"Mount up, JCRs," Jodi called suddenly. "Looks like we've found an animal path. It's plenty wide enough for us to ride. With any luck it will take us to the river."

That made sense to Tommy. He knew that animal paths often led to water.

"Wait a minute, Jodi," Colly said. "I think you should see this." He was holding something in his hand.

Jodi peered closely at it. "Animal hair. Looks like a bear. Where did you find it?"

Colly pointed to the tree next to him.

"Bears tend to rub up against trees," Jodi said. "No problem. I haven't seen any tracks, so it's probably not too fresh."

Colly didn't look satisfied.

"Something else, Colly?"

"No...not really. It's just that it was way up here." He stepped on a rock and tapped on the trunk about six feet up from the ground. "How would a bear rub that high?"

Jodi frowned and sucked in her bottom lip. Finally she shrugged. "Guess it's just another Yukon mystery."

She swung herself back up in her saddle and began leading the way down their new trail.

Tommy was glad this trail was narrow. The last thing he wanted was for Jaz to ride beside him and whisper that the hair might be from a bushman.

Suddenly his hair stood straight up on his neck, and he had a clear and overwhelming feeling that someone was watching them. Someone, or some*thing*! He peered left and then right into the woods on both sides of the trail. Nothing.

His arms were solid gooseflesh. He opened his mouth to warn the others, but then he stopped.

What exactly was he going to say?

He hadn't seen or heard anything. It was just a feeling.

If there *was* something wrong, the horses would sense it, wouldn't they?

His horse didn't seem to notice anything. The other horses looked normal too.

None of the other JCRs seemed concerned. They kept riding steadily forward, rocking in their saddles to the rhythm of the horses.

He glanced left and right again but saw nothing.

So why was his breathing suddenly shallow and quick? Why was his pulse racing? And what was that terrible smell? It was faint, but it was there. It reminded him of the time the power went out back home, and the meat in their freezer had all gone bad.

He looked behind him.

The trail was clear.

He took a deep breath in and let it out again noisily, hoping the sound would distract him from how silly he was being. He couldn't help it. Maybe it was the smell, but all he could think about was their talk around the campfire last night, especially the stuff about the bushman and the windigo. Suddenly a shriek split the air! As if under attack, the horses began rearing. Who had screamed? Was it him? Maybe he'd been so freaked out and jumpy...but he didn't recall opening his mouth.

There was no time to think it through. As Timber began thundering out of control through the woods,

Tommy hunkered down, one hand entwined in her mane, the other clutching the saddle horn in a death grip.

He had to put aside his confusion and blind panic as he quickly turned to the business of hanging on. Whatever had frightened the horses was now far behind them. It hadn't been him—he was sure of that now. It must had been some animal in the woods. Jodi did say that horses were prey animals—no wonder they bolted.

He'd lost hold of his reins, but he remembered what Jodi had told him about riding with his body. His thighs and knees gripped the horse so tightly they ached. He knew the pressure was only going to make Timber run faster, but he was afraid that if he eased up he would fall off.

What had Jodi told them about a runaway horse?

Nothing. She'd only said that her horses had seen pretty much everything and wouldn't scare.

But sometimes it's what you *don't* see that is most frightening.

Timber began to slow down, puffing hard. Tommy let go of the saddle horn and began stroking her neck.

He remembered what Jodi had said about helping a horse when going down a slope. He leaned back to help her go slower. "Whoa, girl," he said.

Timber stopped.

Tommy's wild ride had jiggled his spine into rubber. He slid from Timber's sweaty back and crumpled to the ground, sinking into the moss and sand. He leaned his cheek against the rough bark of a jack-pine tree, appreciating its bite. It meant he was alive.

What about the others?

He struggled to his feet. "Hello!" he shouted.

"Tommy?"

It was Colly, but his voice didn't sound close. How far had his horse bolted? "Colly, I'm over here!"

"Where?"

He glanced about. "I don't know!"

"Come toward my voice."

He moved to where Timber was happily pulling up bunches of grass and picked up her reins. "Come on, girl," he said softly. "This time we're going at *my* speed."

"Tommy!"

"Yeah, I'm coming!" Tommy called.

"I need you to keep talking so I can find you!"

"Oh, right," he muttered. Then he called out loudly, "Right! Sorry!"

"No problem. I think I can see your path."

No doubt. Timber had pushed through whatever was in her way. They were lucky she hadn't hurt herself. Or him.

Suddenly, Timber neighed and shied away from him. Tommy hung on tightly to the reins. He felt the hairs on the back of his neck prickle.

Oh no...not again!

He dropped the reins and whirled around in a circle, vaguely aware of Timber crashing through the woods.

"Where are you?" he yelled, suddenly angry. He didn't know what he was angry at, only that...something...maybe a bear or a wolf, had scared the horses earlier, and he wanted to see it. Horses were afraid of predators. But Tommy knew that most predators were big cowards when it came to humans.

The first thing he noticed was the smell. It was like someone had really bad breath. No, it was worse than that. It reeked of death, like a rotten, maggoty carcass left to bloat in the sun. Then, directly in front of him, leaves rustled and branches parted.

His blood ran cold.

What was staring back at him didn't look like an animal.

It didn't look human either.

Its head was covered in reddish brown hair, but it didn't have a snout like a bear or a wolf, or any other beast he'd ever seen, even in his dreams. It sort of looked human, but not really. Its face was pushed in, but instead of a nose, it had what looked like breathing holes. Its lips were pulled back in a smile, revealing long yellow fangs.

Then he realized it wasn't smiling.

It had no lips!

He shrieked and scrambled backward. Stumbling, he lost sight of the creature. He glanced about, frantic. Where had it gone? And where had Timber gone? No time to search—he took off like a horse, bolting through woods, running helter-skelter wherever his feet could find footing until one toe caught on a rock or a root, and he fell and fell and fell. Everything went black.

When he came to, he opened his eyes to Colly peering down at him too close to his own face. "Get away from me!" he said weakly, pushing his friend and sitting up. His head was throbbing. Looking down, he discovered he'd been resting on a chunk of granite. Some pillow!

"You scared me," Colly said. "I thought I was going to have to give you mouth-to-mouth."

"That *is* scary," Tommy said, attempting to smile. It felt more like a grimace. He looked around. They were in a small clearing, with Timber close by, grazing as if nothing had happened. Tommy opened his mouth to warn Colly about the creature, but stopped. He was no longer certain that he'd seen it at all. Could he have dreamed it when he was knocked unconscious?

He rubbed his aching head. "Was I out long?" he asked.

"I don't think so. It was only thirty seconds or so from the time I last heard you, until I found you. I heard you scream like a little girl. See a bear or something?"

"Yeah, something," Tommy muttered. Then seeing that Colly was frowning, he added, "Nothing. I don't even remember."

Colly gave him a hand up. "Come on, we've got to get back to the others."

"Is everyone okay?"

Colly shook his head. "Jaz thinks she's broken her ankle, but Shelby and Evan are okay. Only Shelby hung on to her horse. And Timber's still here. That means we've got two horses between the five of us."

Tommy nodded, glad that he'd hung on during his wild ride. "Wait," he said. "What about Jodi and her horse?"

Colly shook his head. "We don't know. We called for her, but she's not answering."

Chapter Seven

Colly was quiet as he motioned for Tommy to follow with his horse. That was fine with Tommy. He needed time to think about how their trail ride through the mountains had taken such a terrible turn.

Maybe it was his fault. Perhaps he'd brought some sort of bad luck down on them by not speaking up about the fire when he had a chance.

He gave his head a shake. That was crazy.

So was thinking he'd seen that...*thing* in the woods.

The memory of it made his heart race. He glanced from one side of the trail to the other.

Trees. Only trees.

But if he had imagined or dreamed it, why was he still looking for it?

"Here we are," Colly said.

They entered an open area covered with purple fireweed, slender-leafed Labrador tea and plenty of long wild grass for the horses. Jaz was hopping, with help from Shelby, toward a fallen log. "It's not broken," Tommy heard Shelby say. "But it might be sprained."

Shelby's horse, a golden beast with a creamy mane and tail, was tearing up clumps of grass. It looked up and made a happy rumbling noise as they entered the clearing. Timber made the same happy noise back.

"Any luck?" Colly called to Evan, who had just come back to the clearing. "Evan went to look for Jodi while I was looking for you," he explained to Tommy.

Meeting Tommy and Colly halfway, Evan looked at his feet before speaking.

Tommy felt something icy settle in the pit of his belly. "What is it?" he asked.

Evan cleared his throat. "I found her, but she's not moving."

"So you *left* her?" Tommy cried.

"It's just that...," Evan began. He stopped to swallow. His face was white as milk. The freckles on his cheeks stood out like ink spots. "I think she's dead. Looks like she was thrown where that last rock slide was, and she slid or rolled about thirty feet almost straight down. I couldn't climb down the slide to check, but I could see there's blood, and her body is... look, she's dead, okay?"

Colly looked grim. "Show us," he said. With Evan leading the way, they soon arrived at the rock slide. Afraid to look, but knowing he must, Tommy peered down the slide, swallowing the bile that began rising once again. He didn't want to believe she was dead. He couldn't. This had been such a terrible day.

As he leaned over the edge, suddenly it felt like he was falling. Evan pulled him back. "Easy!" Evan said. "You just about took a dive down the cliff!"

"Sorry, man," Tommy croaked. "This headache is making me a bit dizzy."

"Yeah...headache," Colly said. "Ever think you might have a concussion? Maybe you hit your head harder than you thought when you knocked yourself out."

"Maybe," Tommy said.

Tommy, Evan and Colly leaned over the edge again, except this time Colly had a firm grip on Tommy's shoulder.

Tommy blinked, not sure what he should be seeing.

"Where'd she go?" Evan sounded confused.

"Are you sure you saw her?" Colly asked.

"Yes, I'm sure." Evan was pacing along the edge of the slide, looking down from different angles. He turned and faced Colly and Tommy. "I wasn't imagining her lying there. I *couldn't* have imagined it!"

"She must be okay after all," Tommy said.

"Yeah...," Colly said, his brow creased. "But where is she?"

Evan scowled at Colly. "You don't believe me."

"I'm not saying that, it's just..."

Tommy could see both of his friends were becoming upset. "Hey, take it easy," he said. "Lots of mysteries in the Yukon, remember? Jodi said that. Let's just be glad she isn't dead. Maybe she hit her head and can't remember anything. She probably wandered off or something."

"Yeah, maybe that's it," Evan said.

Colly nodded. "We've got to find her."

They jogged back to the clearing. As soon as Shelby heard about Tommy almost going over the cliff, she insisted on checking him out. She held his head steady, pinching his chin between her thumb and forefinger as Colly and Evan told what they had—and hadn't—seen.

"What do you mean, she isn't there?" Shelby asked, peering into Tommy's eyes. Her closeness was making him feel twitchy.

"Hey...mind giving me a little space?"

"I'm looking at your eyeballs to see if they wander," she explained. "I saw it on TV. If they wander, you have a concussion."

"I'm fine."

"You almost passed out again," Colly said.

"Only because I was leaning over, and my head hurts so bad."

"Exactly," Shelby said. "Possible concussion." She stood. "So where is she? Jodi, I mean."

Evan shrugged. "We don't know. It's like she just evaporated."

"But if she's not hurt, why hasn't she found us?" Tommy asked.

"Maybe her horse ran a long way," Jaz offered.

Colly shook his head. "Her horse was jumpier than ours, but Jodi pretty much lives in the saddle. I can't see a horse getting away from her."

They all fell silent, as if not wanting to speak their thoughts.

"Should we wait?" Shelby asked, finally. "Either Jodi will find us or someone else will when we don't come back."

"No one will even be looking for us for another few hours," Colly said. "When they do, they won't know we took this trail. And what if Jodi really did lose her memory? The sooner we look for her the better."

The thought of the five of them wandering through these woods left Tommy cold. He had to tell them what he'd seen.

"Hey, guys?" Tommy began. His voice cracked, and he coughed to clear it. They might laugh at him, or think him crazy, but he had to warn them. "I think I should tell you something."

"It's about time!" Jaz, still sitting on her fallen log. "You've been a cranky-pants all morning. I knew something was bugging you!"

"No...nothing is bugging me, Jaz," he lied, wondering if his guilt was painted on his face like

Halloween makeup. "It's just that I saw something before Colly found me."

"What?" Colly asked.

Tommy took a deep breath and let it out. He stared at his hands as he spoke. "I know this is going to sound crazy, but I think I saw a bushman."

Chapter Eight

Out of the corner of his eye Tommy saw Jaz sit up straighter. "Before I saw it, I could feel it watching, and I smelled it. It was following us."

"When?" Shelby asked.

"As soon as we started up the Crank."

"That can't be right," Jaz said. "Because I saw the bushman at the top of the Crank when we were still down at the river."

"Are you guys kidding me?" Colly said. "There was no bushman!"

"Was too," Jaz said. "But I knew you wouldn't believe me."

"There *are* bushmen, Colly," Evan said. "There have always been stories about them."

Colly was shaking his head. "This is crazy."

"But," Evan continued, "if Jaz saw the same creature at the top of the Crank as Tommy did at the bottom, it might have been a windigo. A windigo moves at lightning speed through the woods. If Tommy says it was following us, that could mean it's on the hunt."

"And then there was the scream," Tommy said.

"What scream?" Jaz asked.

"You must have heard it," he said. "It scared the horses!"

The others frowned and shook their heads.

"I don't think any of us heard it," Evan said. "If you were the only one who heard a windigo scream, that could be very bad for you."

Tommy felt like he was going to throw up. He was glad the others didn't think he was crazy—well, except Colly. But he was not glad that what he saw in the woods might be a windigo. He swallowed hard.

Shelby turned to Tommy. "What did it look like?"

He shuddered and wrapped his arms around his stomach to try and settle himself. "Yellow teeth...long. H-hairy face," he stuttered.

"Sure sounds like a windigo," Evan said.

"Or a bushman," Jaz said.

"Some people think they are the same," Shelby reminded them.

"This is all very interesting," Colly said. "But we still need to find Jodi before she hurts herself or gets deeper into the woods."

"That's if she's really lost her memory," Evan said.

"If she didn't, why isn't she looking for us?" Jaz asked.

Shelby frowned. "Maybe she is looking for us, but went the wrong way."

"We'd better get moving," Colly said.

"She must have left tracks," Evan said, standing. "How shall we do this?"

"I can't walk," Jaz said. "And I don't want to ride in case my ankle gets bumped. Maybe it's not broken, but it really, *really* hurts!"

Shelby put her hand on Jaz's shoulder. "Okay, Jaz and I will stay here in case Jodi comes back this way."

"What about the bushman or windigo or whatever it is!" Jaz cried. "I don't want it to get us!"

Tommy gulped. "Don't worry, Jaz. If I'm the only one who heard the scream, maybe I'm the one the windigo is after."

"Oh, for crying out loud!" Colly said. "I don't know what you think you saw, Tommy, but remember you had a pretty good conk on the head. We're not going to find anything in these woods except Jodi. Okay?"

Jaz looked tearful.

"You guys look, and Jaz and I will stay here," Shelby said. She turned to Jaz. "I'll build a fire to keep any animals away. Plus, the old stories say fire is the one thing that will destroy a windigo, so the fire will keep it away too. Okay?"

After a moment, Jaz nodded. She looked at Tommy. "You be careful!"

"Of course," he said. He wished he felt as sure as he sounded.

He didn't like the idea of leaving Jaz and Shelby, but he felt an overwhelming urge to run as fast and as far as he could. There was something very wrong about this place. He could feel it.

He snorted at his own foolishness.

Jaz and Shelby would be fine until they returned. Of course they would.

Uncertain what kind of terrain they would be heading into, they decided they would be better off on foot than riding. Leaving the horses with Shelby and

Jaz, they walked back to the place Jodi's body should have been and slid down the side of the mountain to take a closer look. There were blood splatters on the stones and a wide trail scraped in the dirt and stone. Tommy saw his own confusion reflected in the faces of his friends.

"It looks like she dragged something," Colly said.

"Maybe it was her oilskin coat?" Evan asked. "It looked heavy."

"Heavy enough to do this?" Tommy asked.

There were no answers, so they began checking the woods, trying to determine which way she'd gone.

Evan let out a breath. He sounded frustrated. "Well, if she was dragging something, she stopped doing it when she left the slide. I can't tell where she went."

Tommy was feeling sweaty, and his head, in spite of what he'd told the others, was throbbing. Urgency was building in the pit of his belly as he thought of the creature that might be hunting him. The memory of it left his mouth dry. "Look, we know the river is down at the bottom," he said. "Jodi was taking us that way before the slide happened, so maybe she is heading there now. We should check it out. Now!"

Colly frowned at him. He looked like he was going to say something, but before he could speak Evan called from where he'd been searching.

"Over here!"

"You found her trail?" Colly asked.

"I found *a* trail. I don't know if it's the right one, but if Jodi's on it we should be able to catch up with her pretty quick."

Tommy felt a surge of hope.

They jogged in single file, occasionally calling out for Jodi. Once they spotted bear scat, but it wasn't fresh. Tommy touched the back of his neck to make sure the hair wasn't standing up. Once, he thought he heard a shout, but it was from far off, and he couldn't be sure he'd heard anything at all. He strained his ears, afraid of what he might hear but also afraid of what he might *not* hear. What if the monster decided to grab them without warning?

Abruptly, the path ended in a rock face, twenty feet straight up.

"Oh, *man*!" Tommy cried.

"Don't worry," Evan said. "We were going too fast. There must have been another path. We just didn't see it."

They turned, this time with Tommy in the lead. All he wanted to do was run, but they couldn't afford to miss finding the path. As much as he hated it, they had to slow down.

As they walked and searched, he took deep breaths. Something in Tommy's soul drank in the tang of pine, the smell of the earth. This was a place where a person could go to forget and be forgotten about. Here, with the canopy of trees locking piney fingers high above him, it was like he was in another world—one far away from the fire at camp and his guilty conscience. His neck prickled.

This time he didn't wait. Like a prey animal, he bolted.

Chapter Nine

"Tommy!" he heard Colly shout.

He couldn't stop. He couldn't think. All he knew—all he felt—was terror. It blanketed him, smothered him, tried to suck him down. He had to get away!

It was the monster! Behind him, he could hear it panting. He could feel its hot breath on his neck.

Oh no!

Somehow he'd circled back to the cliff where they'd looked for Jodi—but he was going too fast! He tried to slide to a stop, but couldn't, and in a breath was over the edge, twisting his body in the air, grasping for anything. His fingers locked on roots. *Hang on!* he willed them. *Please hang on!*

His head was pounding. It hurt so much he thought his eyes would pop out of his skull. His fingers were sweaty, and he was losing his grip.

Suddenly a hand clasped one of his and with incredible strength pulled him back up from the precipice.

It wasn't Colly.

It wasn't Evan.

It was huge, and its face was almost completely covered in hair!

It was the monster he'd seen the woods!

Or was it?

As far as monsters go, this one wasn't very scary. It was more like a very hairy man.

As Tommy crumpled to the ground, chest heaving, the bushman turned and disappeared into the woods.

"Wait!" Tommy cried as he tried to stand.

Colly and Evan burst through the brush.

"Tommy!" Colly cried. "Are you crazy? Did you get stung by a bee or something?"

"Come on!" Tommy croaked, motioning for the others to follow. "It's the bushman. It saved me."

Evan's eyes were as big as tennis balls. "A windigo saved you?"

"No, it wasn't a windigo...come on!"

The bushman was moving fast, but Tommy could still see flashes of blue. The monster was wearing a blue shirt.

Tommy and Evan must have seen it too. They joined him in his pursuit. Evan grabbed Tommy's arm, helping him stay upright.

The bushman had come and gone so quickly, Tommy's mind was still trying to catch up to what his eyes had seen.

He remembered the flashes of blue he'd seen earlier on the trail. Could it have been this creature and its shirt?

At one point it turned, aware that they were following, and waved its hairy arms about its head, as if threatening them. As soon as they stopped, it turned and continued on its path.

"If it's a bushman, we're nuts to follow," Evan said.

"Since when do bushmen wear clothes?" Colly asked.

"How do you know that they don't?"

"I doubt it's a bushman," Colly said, "but if this guy saved Tommy, he can't be all bad. Maybe he can help us. Let's go!"

They resumed their chase. "If it's not a bushman," Evan puffed, "it's the biggest, fastest guy I've ever seen!"

Tommy's ears told him they were nearing water. The creature disappeared down a path around a more heavily treed bend. They ran faster, and the path opened into a small clearing. Tommy, Colly and Evan stumbled to a stop, blinking at each other, wide-eyed.

Timber was at the edge of the clearing, minus her saddle and bridle, in what looked like a makeshift corral. Shelby's horse was there too. Their saddles were resting on the ground just outside.

The bushman was walking toward a waterfall on the side of a rock face. When he reached the waterfall, he didn't slow his pace, but walked right though it!

"Did we just see that?" Colly asked.

Tommy nodded. "Uh-huh."

"Come on, you guys," Evan said. "I bet there's a passage into the mountain behind there."

Tommy and Colly looked at each other. Colly shrugged, as if to say, "This guy knows about mountains. I don't."

Tommy didn't know about mountains either.

Cautiously, they approached the waterfall. Up close, where the water splashed down the mountain's granite face, they could see that it might have an open space behind. Tommy put his hand into the stream and pushed it through. It *was* open.

Without waiting to see if the others would follow, he plunged through the wall of water. It soaked and refreshed him, though his head was still aching.

On the other side, he stood, open-mouthed. A few seconds later, Colly and Evan joined him.

They were standing in what looked like someone's primitive mudroom. There were sharpened sticks and an assortment of tools. To one side, leaning against the stone wall were what looked like homemade snowshoes. A pile of neatly stacked chopped wood was piled close to where the passageway turned. They could see by the light that came from outdoors—from behind the tumbling water. But there was another glow of light after a bend in the passage. It was a warmer light. It looked man-made.

"Well, come on, then," a gruff voice called.

Tommy could see the whites of his friends' eyes. Evan shrugged, as if to say, "We might as well..."

Around the bend they saw the "bushman" sitting on a stool. He was not a monster. A giant, yes, but most definitely a man. Even sitting he looked like he was taller than any basketball player. His hair flowed down to his waist and was the color of decaying leaves. His eyebrows were so bushy they appeared to grow out of his beard, which was sprouting from almost every part of his face. Body hair bristled from the opening of his worn, blue shirt, and Tommy could see that his arms were hairy as well. If this was the guy Jaz had seen on the mountain, it was easy to see why she had thought he was a bushman.

"Hi, guys!"

Startled, Tommy glanced to the side of the dim cavern and could feel Colly's and Evan's heads swivel along with his. It was Jaz! In a blink he could see that Shelby and Jodi were there too. Shelby and Jaz were leaning against a wall stacked with cartons, and it looked like their hands and feet were tied. Jodi was lying on a table.

Tommy blinked, trying to make sense of what he was seeing. It was as if Jodi was sleeping. There was a blanket underneath her, and a pillow under her head. Her head was bandaged with strips of yellow cloth.

For a moment he wondered if she was dead. Maybe Evan had been right!

Suddenly she moaned and moved her head just a little. Tommy noticed there was another strip of cloth wrapped entirely around her and the tabletop, as if meant to hold her in place.

"I think she's in a coma," Jaz said softly.

Tommy looked back at Jaz and realized she wasn't as cheerful as her hello had sounded. Her face was pinched, and her eyes were wide. "Don't talk!" the bushman shouted at Jaz.

Before Tommy, Colly and Evan could react, the giant moved behind them, cutting off their escape.

Chapter Ten

For a split second, Tommy, Colly and Evan stood as if frozen. Tommy recovered his voice first. "What's going on?" he croaked. "Is Jodi okay?"

Without answering, and without moving away from the opening, the man pulled two lengths of rope from one of the crates set against the wall. He handed them to Colly. "Tie him up," he said, motioning toward Evan. "No funny stuff."

Tommy gulped as the man moved his shirttail to show a huge knife hanging from his rope belt. It didn't look like a very safe way to carry something like that. At the moment it was especially unsafe for Jodi and the JCRs.

When Colly finished tying Evan, the man handed another two loops of rope to Tommy and made him tie Colly's wrists and ankles. Tommy tried not to tie the knots too tight, but catching a warning glance from the man, he didn't tie them too loose either.

When Tommy finished with Colly, the man motioned for him to sit and hold out his own hands and feet. Tommy was relieved the man didn't tie him too tight. He was also confused. Why were they being tied up? Were they being kidnapped? It seemed strange for this man to save Tommy from going over the cliff and then take him—and the others—hostage. After the man's gruff command, Tommy was afraid to say anything. He exchanged glances with the other JCRs, and guessed they were feeling the same way.

The bushman moved to where Jodi lay and stared down at her.

The silence was killing Tommy. He had to know what the man had planned for them! "Please," he said, finally. "Tell us why you tied us up." He tried to speak calmly, even though he felt anything but. The man shook his head. He didn't take his eyes off Jodi.

"Why not?" Jaz asked.

The hairy man waved his hand at her, as if trying to push away her words. She exchanged a glance with Tommy and shrugged.

"Look, you can't just tie us up and not expect us to ask questions," Tommy said. The man still wouldn't look at him. Tommy's blood suddenly ran cold. "Are you some kind of a psycho-murderer?"

The man moved so fast that Tommy barely had time to register that he was right in front of him. "I'm not a murderer!" he growled.

Looking into the man's eyes, Tommy gulped. They were angry eyes, but also shocked, like he couldn't believe Tommy would say such a thing. After a moment, the man shrugged and shook his head. Tommy breathed again. With a start he realized his headache was much better. Maybe it was like when you have a sore foot, and you hit your thumb with a hammer. Suddenly your foot doesn't seem as sore.

The man returned to the table and stared at Jodi.

The JCRs looked at each other, bewildered.

After a minute, the man turned to the JCRs. "Got somethin' I can read?" he asked. One by one, they shook their heads—except for Jodi, who still appeared to be asleep. Was Jaz right? Could she be in a coma?

As if in answer, Jodi groaned again. Tommy was pretty sure that when people were in comas, they didn't make any sounds. He was relieved that she was alive, but if she was unconscious, she could be seriously injured.

The man sighed heavily and looked at his toes. His feet were wrapped in what looked like kamiks, traditional boots of the Inuit, except that they were shorter and not very well stitched together. Tommy guessed he had made them himself. His pants looked the same way. His shirt looked like it came from a store, but it was obviously too small. He'd split the sleeves up the arms, so that they hung in flaps, and he only had a couple of the buttons done up.

This was all so strange. They were the man's prisoners, and yet he seemed desperate for them to know he hadn't killed anyone. It would make more sense for him to want them to think he was a psycho-murderer in order to keep them afraid.

"I'm sorry if I said something wrong," Tommy offered.

"S'okay," the man said. "It's just that you reminded me of what happened to poor Bettyanne. I didn't kill her, you know."

"Who's Bettyanne?" Evan asked.

Instead of answering, the man took out the large knife he carried at his side and began scraping it in the dirt. He appeared to be lost in thought. Colly and Evan looked at each other. Colly shrugged and cleared his throat. "Can you tell us who you are?"

The hairy man blinked, as if for a moment he'd forgotten they were there. "Name's Albert Payne," he said.

Colly frowned. "Should we know you?"

"You don't know me."

"Your name…it sounds familiar."

"You don't know me!" Albert snapped. "Everyone thinks they know what I did, but I didn't do it! I didn't kill Bettyanne. It weren't me!"

Albert jumped to his feet and began pacing back and forth in the small space, muttering.

"It's okay, Albert," Shelby said, keeping her voice soft and steady, as if she was calming a spooked beast. "We didn't mean to upset you."

He looked sharply at her but didn't say anything.

"Is it okay if I call you Albert?" Tommy tried.

Albert looked at him and shrugged. "Sure…go ahead," he said. "You and me is tied. I guess we should be friendly."

Tommy frowned. "I know *I'm* tied, but you look pretty free to me."

"What's your name?" Albert asked.

Tommy hesitated, but only for a second. "Tommy," he said. He didn't think it would make any difference if the guy knew his real name. Besides, why lie? He'd done enough of that lately. If his lying really had brought them bad luck, maybe it was time to try something else. They could really use some good luck about now.

"Hello, Tommy. I used to read a lot, you know." Albert began pacing again, but this time he looked calmer, hands clasped behind his back. "I liked lots of different kinds of books. I liked mysteries and war stories, and even those romance-type books my wife used to buy at the flea market."

Once again, he moved to the table and looked down at Jodi. After a moment, he turned back to Tommy. "I once read that if you save someone's life you end up tied to them for as long as you both live," he said.

Tommy cleared his throat. "So you're saying that you and I are tied because you saved me from falling off that cliff?" he asked. "But if you saved me, why did you tie me and my friends up?" He took a chance. "And who is Bettyanne?"

"Got it!" Colly cried. "You're that guy we heard about—the one that murdered his wife's friend and took off into the woods!" It was the story Colly had shared during their campfire. "But that was ten years ago. Have you been here the whole time?"

Once again Albert looked upset. "It weren't me!" he shouted and began stomping his foot like a three-year-old having a tantrum. "Everyone thinks I'm the one what did it, but it weren't me!"

When he finally stopped, Tommy took a big breath. "It's okay, Albert. If you want, you can tell us what really happened."

"Thank you," Albert mumbled, rubbing his forehead. "Sorry I got so mad."

"So who killed Bettyanne?" Jaz asked.

Albert gave her a bitter look. "My wife!"

Chapter Eleven

"That wife of mine...nuthin' but trouble!" Albert muttered, walking round and round in circles. Whatever else he was saying decomposed into a series of angry mutterings Tommy could make no sense of.

"The story we heard is that you had some sort of fight with your wife's friend, and you shot her," Colly said. "That's what it said in the old newspaper I looked at anyway. It didn't say much else, other than that you took off and that no one could find you."

Albert stopped his pacing and moved to one of his crates. After a moment he pulled out a rifle and held it above his head. Tommy froze. The others stayed silent.

"Sure," Albert said. "They said I was the one what did it. With this." He lifted the rifle up and down above his head as if he was in a gym, pumping iron. "Except this gun weren't mine. It were my wife's. Made special, on account of her being a southpaw."

"So," Colly said. "You're saying your wife is left-handed, and that she shot Bettyanne with this special left-handed rifle."

"Yup."

"Why?" Tommy asked.

Albert drew in a deep breath and let it out. "Me and Bettyanne were planning a surprise party for her big brother, who was my best friend. My wife walked in and saw Bettyanne making sketches of how she wanted to decorate the room. Saphire—that's my wife—thought we were planning on knocking over a bank and cutting her out."

"Why would she think that?" Tommy asked.

Albert shrugged. "Dunno. She used to run with a bad crowd. She promised she would be a good girl after she married me, but she never stopped thinking bad things." He sighed. "Anyway, she only meant to show us she meant business, but the gun went off." Albert sat on the floor, legs crossed, and hung his head, sniffling. "She said she didn't mean it and she was so sorry. She asked me to help her by taking away the gun. I knew it were wrong, but I did it anyway. I took the gun into the woods, and when I found this cave I knew it would be a perfect hiding place. But on my way back to town, I snuck past two guys fishing, and they was talking about how I done it, and how the police was looking for me." He shook his head, sadly. "Saphire told them it were me. I didn't know what to do, so I took off."

"Have you been here all this time?" Jaz asked.

"Here and there," Albert said. "Mostly here. Had to scare some people. Let them think I was a bushman." Suddenly he stood and walked toward Jodi. "But *she* were the big liar!" he spat, staring down at her. "She told them I did it!"

So Jaz was right. She really *had* seen something on the mountain, but it wasn't really a bushman. It was Albert. "Why didn't you just tell the truth?" Tommy asked, thinking of his own secret.

"How could I?" Albert cried. "No one would have believed me. And that poor Bettyanne! When I first took off, it was to hide from the police just long enough to sort things in my head, you know? I didn't plan on staying away, but the more time passes, the harder it is to unknot a lie."

"But you have the gun as proof," Tommy said. "You can go back now. Tell the truth. We believe you..." He looked to the others, who all nodded their heads. "You don't have to keep living like this."

Albert sighed. "The thing about a lie is it can get so big that you can't get back around it."

Tommy thought about his own lie. He realized that going to Captain Conrad now would be even harder than before. Wouldn't it be easier to just leave it? Unlike Albert, however, they couldn't stay on the mountain. "What about Jodi?" he asked. "She's hurt. We've got to get her to a doctor."

At first Albert didn't seem that he'd heard. Finally, in a voice barely louder than a whisper he said, "That her name? Jodi? She reminds me of her, you know."

"Who?" Evan asked.

"Saphire. My wife."

Tommy's blood ran cold.

Saphire obviously wasn't Albert's favorite person. Would he hurt Jodi?

Tommy looked at his friends and saw his concern reflected in their eyes.

Albert moved to a barrel at the side of the cave. He picked up a bowl and a cloth and dipped the bowl in the barrel. Then he moved back to Jodi, dipped the cloth in the bowl and began wiping her face. He was humming. Tommy relaxed. It was clear Albert only wanted to help Jodi. But why? What would he do if she recovered? Would he keep her tied up like the rest of them? And if they were being held hostage, shouldn't he be writing some sort of a ransom note?

Tommy felt Colly lean close. "Your ropes are loose," he whispered. "You've got to make a run for it."

Tommy shook his head, checking first to make sure Albert hadn't noticed.

Albert had his back to them and was still wiping Jodi's face.

"There's no way I'm leaving without you guys!"

"You're the only one with a chance." Colly sounded grim.

It was true, but as he looked at Albert's long legs, he didn't think much of that chance.

"You said you're not a murderer, and I believe you," Shelby said, her voice surprisingly steady. "It's nice that you're trying to help Jodi, but...we don't understand why you would help us, and then just keep us here."

"That's all you plan on doing, right?" Jaz squeaked. "You're not planning on...killing us?"

Tommy held his breath, and he was sure the others were doing the same.

"I guess that's the tricky bit," Albert said, scratching his head. "I didn't plan on any of this, but that woman there," he said, nodding toward Jodi, "I could see she needed help. Then I started thinking about the rest of you, and figured I'd better check on you. That one there"—he nodded to Jaz—"saw me and started shouting that I was a windigo, so I figured I'd better bring her and the other girl here too."

"So why didn't you bring me back here after you saved me?" Tommy asked.

"I dunno," Albert said. "All I was thinking was that we was tied, so I owed you. I'm not sure if that's a rule or not, but I figured you didn't get a good enough look at me to know anything. But then you and them others followed me. Guess it was meant to be."

"No way!" Evan cried. "Killing innocent people is never meant to be."

"I haven't decided on the killing," Albert muttered. "Not yet anyway." He walked back over to Jodi, picked up the bowl and returned to wiping her face and humming.

While Albert's back was turned, Colly gave Tommy a nudge. He nodded and began wiggling his feet, trying to loosen the ropes. He exchanged a quick elated glance with Colly as his pulled one foot free.

The others saw as well.

Evan mouthed "Now!" at Tommy.

He thought it was a crazy plan, but it was also their only chance. With Albert busy caring for Jodi, he slipped out the cave entrance and under the waterfall to the outside.

Chapter Twelve

His hands were only loosely tied, but he didn't have time to free them. He would do that as he ran! At least they were tied in front of him, so he could protect himself if he fell.

He heard Timber nicker at him from the pen.

"Sorry, girl," he whispered as he ran past her. His only chance was to get out of sight—fast. He knew he only had seconds before Albert noticed he was gone.

He slipped into the bush at the far end of the clearing, the opposite side from where he, Colly and Evan had entered a short time ago.

Sure enough, he heard a roar from inside the cave. He wasn't about to stick around and see Albert come out!

As quickly and as quietly as he could, he snaked into the bush, trying not to break branches or to step where he would leave tracks. His head was pounding again, drowning out the beat of his heart and the rush of his breath, which he was trying hard to control. With a stitch in his side, he ran on, and on, until he could go no farther. He let himself fall into a bed of moss and fireweed.

His face felt hot. His side felt like it was being ripped in two. His head felt like it would crack like an eggshell, it hurt so bad. He breathed deeply, in and out, and eventually caught his breath. The pounding in his head eased, and he was able to listen for Albert. As he listened, he slowly loosened the ropes around his wrists.

He could hear the buzz of flying insects and birds in the woods, but nothing that sounded like it might be Albert.

Was it possible? Had he lost him?

Hands now free, he sat up, listening hard.

Bugs. Birds. Nothing more.

But…there was…something. He sniffed. What was that smell? He leaned close to the fireweed. It smelled more like really rotting meat than a flower.

His blood ran cold as he remembered where he'd smelled it before.

The windigo!

In a flash, he was on his feet and running again. He didn't know where he was going, and he didn't care what kind of trail he was leaving. All he knew was that he had to get away! He tore through the brush, hardly noticing willow saplings whipping against his face and arms.

"Stop!" Albert shouted, as Tommy barreled into his stomach. Albert had found him. Tommy fell back onto the ground, peering anxiously around him like a cornered animal. "Sheesh, kid, calm down!"

He took deep breaths in and out. "Okay," he panted, still looking around, silently cursing himself. His crazy running had gotten him caught again. Why had he been so spooked? From a smell? He shook his head at his own stupidity. He'd let the others down. Again. He glanced anxiously at his captor, wondering how angry Albert would be at him for running.

He didn't look angry. Just concerned. Concern looked strange on a wild man who was keeping five JCRs and a horse wrangler captive. It wasn't what Tommy expected.

"Not good to be out here on your own," Albert growled, peering into the woods. He took a firm hold of Tommy's arm and walked him through the brush. Before long they were back in the clearing by the cave. It looked to Tommy like he must have gone in a circle. Timber nickered as they went past her and back through the waterfall.

"Hi, guys," he mumbled, eyes down as he entered the cavern.

No one said a word.

Albert pushed him gently, but firmly, back to where he'd been sitting before his escape. He picked up the rope Tommy had squirmed out of, and this time lashed his hands to his ankles. It wasn't very comfortable, but Tommy guessed he deserved that. Next, Albert pulled up a rickety stool and sat in front of him.

"Why'd you run, kid?"

"To get help," Tommy said, his voice small.

"What were you thinking? That you'd save your own skin and leave your friends?"

"No!" he cried.

"I told him to go," Colly said.

Tommy looked at his friend. If Colly was disappointed in him, he wasn't showing it. He glanced at the others. They looked the same as they did before. Anxious.

Albert turned to Evan, Shelby and Jaz. "That true?" he asked. They nodded. He turned back to Tommy. "You were scared of something out there, and it weren't me. What was it?"

Tommy licked his lips. His friends were going think he was an idiot. "You've heard of the windigo, right?"

"Sure," Albert said. To Tommy he sounded a bit nervous.

He swallowed. "Do you think there's a windigo in these woods?"

"I couldn't say," Albert said. "And neither should you! Don't you know it's bad luck to talk about such things?"

"So, you don't think I'm crazy?"

Albert shook his head and stared at his hands. "I been in the woods a long time, and I seen some strange stuff. Lately, the huntin' isn't so good, which means I got to steal food from camps. And the other day I found a bear carcass with its inside ripped out.

Its head was torn away and stuck high up in a tree!" He looked at Tommy, his eyebrows in bushy, upside-down *V*s. "What kind of creature can do that?"

Tommy felt a surge of gratitude that he wasn't alone in thinking there was something really bad out there. He was still terrified of what might be in the woods, but suddenly, Albert didn't seem so scary. "You don't really want to hurt us, do you?" Tommy asked.

"No. Course I don't."

Tommy felt a weight leave him. He didn't know if Albert was being honest, but hearing the words made him feel better. "So what's going to happen to us?"

"Like I said before. That's the tricky bit."

Shelby cleared her throat. "Jodi needs a doctor."

"She's in a coma," Albert said. "Doctors can't do nothing."

"Of course they can," Evan said.

"Besides," Tommy said. "I don't think it's a coma."

As if on cue, Jodi began moaning.

In two steps, Albert was at her side.

Jodi blinked and looked up at Albert; then she turned her head, taking in the JCRs and the cavern.

"What...?" she gasped. She looked back at Albert and pushed herself up off the table, letting loose a string of angry curse words.

Albert held her arms, as Jodi started flailing and hitting him. Then, as if she'd suddenly run out of batteries, she sank back down.

"There," Albert said. "Now she looks like my wife again."

Chapter Thirteen

Albert took a soiled rag out of a back pocket and wiped his forehead. Then he found some rope and tied Jodi's hands. "And now," he announced, "we die."

All of the JCRs began shouting at once. Albert waved his hands to shush them. "I've got dynamite from the gold mine; it'll happen real quick. You won't suffer."

Once again, they all began shouting.

"You can't do this!" Tommy cried. "You're not a murderer, remember?"

Albert stopped and looked at him. The others hushed. "I didn't used to be, but things happen, and you can't go back."

"But you weren't guilty."

"People think I am. If the newspaper says I'm guilty of one thing, I might as well be guilty of another."

"That doesn't make any sense," Colly said. "You can still go back and set the record straight. But if you kill us…murder is something you can never take back."

"I'll be dead too. Why should I care?"

It sounded like he really wanted to know.

Tommy felt something flare inside of him. It was hope. "Please, don't hurt my friends," he pleaded. "This isn't their fault."

"They shouldn'ta come," Albert said. "Sometimes the only way to fix a thing is to bury it."

"Is that what you think you're doing?" Tommy asked. "Fixing things?"

"This is crazy!" Colly said.

"You stay quiet!" Albert roared. He swept his arm around the room to point at all of them. "All of you. Quiet!"

Albert turned back to Tommy and looked at him as if he was waiting.

Tommy swallowed. "Why can't you go back? I mean, *really*," he asked. "Is it because you're afraid they won't believe you? You used to read a lot, so you must know about DNA evidence. You know they can probably match that gun to your wife. Right?"

Albert took a breath. "I can't," he said, his voice cracking. "Don't you see? Everyone said Saphire was gonna be bad for me. Everyone! Even my best friend. He was right, but how can I ever tell him how right he was?"

"So...you're ashamed?"

Head hanging down to his chin, Albert nodded.

Tommy thought for a moment. "But it isn't *your* shame. It's Saphire's."

Albert shrugged. "After all this time, it's the same difference. Shoulda just faced up to things way back when it happened, I guess. Too late now."

"It's *not* too late!"

Tommy felt a prickle on the back of his neck and glanced at the shadows. He licked his lips and swallowed, hard. "I have shame too," he said. He felt his friends staring at him.

"You?" Albert asked. To Tommy he sounded almost hopeful.

It was the lie that had turned Albert into a monster. Tommy knew that telling his own truth, confessing his shame, might be the only way to reach him.

"I did something that really messed things up," he said, his voice barely more than a whisper. He coughed and spoke louder. "I should have admitted it, but I didn't. I let everyone think it was someone else." Staring hard at his feet, he could feel his friends looking at him, but he didn't look up. He couldn't.

He had to confess. More than that, he *wanted* to. Not only to convince Albert, but because this thing inside him, this lie, was changing him. He glanced at Albert, wondering what he must have looked like before he buried himself in this mountain. He'd said he used to like to read books. Tommy imagined him sitting in a large chair, reading, maybe wearing slippers and drinking tea.

He took another deep breath. "I started a fire back at our camp. It was an accident, but it was my fault. One building burned to the ground and another one was damaged. I let a homeless guy take the blame."

There. It was out.

"You didn't tell no one?" Albert asked.

"I was ashamed. And afraid."

"Of what?"

"I was afraid people would think I was some kind of stupid jerk. I was afraid they'd hate me."

"That it?"

Tommy swallowed. "Pretty much. I also told myself that if the people who owned the camp knew what really happened, that they wouldn't let us use the camp again...but that was just an excuse."

Albert sighed deeply, as if a weight had been lifted from him. A small one anyway. Tommy felt it too. He looked at each of his friends They looked confused. And anxious. And hopeful.

He looked at Albert, who appeared to be deep in thought.

"It were good you told the truth," he said, finally. "It were good that these folks could hear it." He looked at each of them. "Do you hate him?"

They all answered at once. Tommy could hardly make sense of what they were saying.

"Course not..."

"Accident..."

"No way..."

"Stupid jerk..."

"Did...someone just call me a stupid jerk?" he asked.

"I said you are *not* a stupid jerk," Colly said. "But you should have trusted us. We're your friends."

"Of course we are!" Jaz said.

"We would have gone with you to tell Captain Conrad," Shelby said.

Albert shook his head. "But it were wrong to let someone else take the blame. Really wrong."

Tommy hung his head. "I know." He looked up. "Please. I have to make it right. I have to tell Captain Conrad that it was my fault."

Albert looked at his feet for a long time. Tommy wondered if he'd gone to sleep. Before he could open his mouth to ask him, the man suddenly stood, walked to Tommy and removed the rope from his wrists and ankles. "Untie them others," he said. "Go!"

He turned and faced the corner, as Tommy raced to untie everyone's wrists and feet. Each helped one of the others as soon as they were free.

Tommy and Shelby moved over to Jodi. "What about her?" Tommy asked.

"I'll look after her," Albert said.

Again, alarm flared. Was he getting Jodi mixed up with his wife who betrayed him? What if he refused to let her go?

Chapter Fourteen

"Albert, this is Jodi," Tommy said softly. "She's not your wife."

Albert frowned. "I know that, kid. I mean I can make something you can pull her on—a travois—and you can hitch it to one of your horses. Probably best not to try and wake her." He rubbed his arm where Jodi had whacked him, and Tommy wasn't sure if Albert meant best for Jodi or best for himself.

Outside, in the glorious sunshine, Jaz stroked Timber's nose, and Evan was retrieving the saddles. Albert was as good as his word. He fashioned a travois by taking wooden poles from a stack near the cave entrance, crossing two of them near their top, and then attaching shorter ones across the middle. It sort of looked like a sloppy letter *A*. He fastened a blanket to make a place for Jodi to ride on, and then used rope to attach it to Shelby's horse, which he deemed the calmer of the two. He walked her back and forth in the clearing until the horse got used to it, and until he was sure she wouldn't spook. Then he disappeared back inside the cave. A moment later he returned with Jodi cradled in his arms. He settled her in the travois and began walking back to the cave.

"Wait!" Tommy said, jogging to catch up with him. He glanced over his shoulder and saw the others hadn't moved. No one tried to follow.

"You'd best be going," Albert said, stopping near the waterfall.

"You're not coming?" Tommy asked.

"Nope. My life down there ended a long time ago."

Tommy shivered as he remembered Albert's plans for blowing up the cave. Surely he wasn't still going to do it! He put his hand on Albert's arm. "You've got to come with us. We're tied, remember?"

Albert looked sad. "No, you can go," he said. "The rule don't make any sense. Time to bury all this, and me, under stone."

Tommy felt a painful lump in his throat. After what he and his friends had just been through, he didn't know why he cared about what happened to this guy, but he did. "Albert, don't talk like that. You can't die. It's because of you that I told the truth about what I did. We *are* tied. You saved my life in two ways. Let me save yours."

"I don't want no saving," Albert said.

"If you die, the lie lives."

Albert sat and put his head in his hands.

"Don't you see?" Tommy asked. "That lie turned you into a bushman monster for all these years. My lie was starting to change me—I could feel it."

"So?"

"Lies make monsters! You have to fix things. How many other people have been affected by this? What happened to your best friend?"

"I don't know," Albert said. He sounded sad.

"Don't you think you should find out? What if you can save him, just like you saved me?"

Albert was shaking his head. "Can't face him."

"Don't you see? You have to! Your wife did this, but maybe your friend has been really mad thinking it was you. Being angry can eat you alive."

Albert dropped his head; his long beard hung between his legs.

"You have to put things right!"

With a deep sigh, Albert stood. "Will you write to me when I go to jail?"

Relief washed over Tommy, threatening to turn his knees to jelly. "It might not come to that," he said.

"Yeah, but it might. Will you?"

Tommy smiled. "Of course I will. No matter what."

They joined the others by the horses. Jodi was still unconscious on the travois.

Something occurred to Tommy. "Albert, do you know who everyone is?"

Albert shook his head. "All I know is you and Jodi."

Tommy nodded. "And this is Colly, Jaz, Shelby and Evan."

"Pleased to meet'cha, I guess," Albert mumbled, staring at his feet. "I'm really sorry about everything."

No one looked like they were happy he was there.

"Is he really coming with us?" Jaz asked.

Albert nodded. "Only if you don't mind. I want to tell the truth."

The others looked at each other. "I guess it's okay," Shelby said.

The horses were ready to go. Jaz still had a sore foot, so she was already on top of Timber. Evan was leading Shelby's horse, which didn't seem the least bit concerned about pulling Jodi behind it. Shelby announced she would walk beside Jodi, to make sure everything stayed okay on that end.

Colly held Timber's reins out for Tommy. "You want to ride with Jaz?" he asked.

"No, you go ahead," Tommy said. "I'll walk with Albert and Evan...as long as Evan doesn't tell any jokes."

As if taking his cue, Evan glanced at Albert and then asked, "When does a horse talk?"

"I don't know. When?" Albert asked, before Tommy could stop him.

"Whinny wants to!"

Everyone groaned, and Colly swung himself into Timber's saddle behind Jaz.

"Wait a minute," Albert said. "I forgot the gun. It's proof, right?" Before Tommy could say anything, Albert ducked back inside the cave. When he returned a moment later, he had a backpack and his gun. He passed the gun to Tommy.

"Don't worry," Albert said. "It isn't loaded."

"Don't you want to carry it?"

"Nope. I'm done with it. Besides, I don't want to make your friends any more nervous than they already are." Without another word he strode out of the clearing and onto the path, the others close behind. He led them along a new path that eventually joined the one they had come up on, well beyond the rock slides.

"The cave was your home for a long time," Tommy said to Albert. "Will you miss it?"

Albert shook his head. "Too much bad stuff in there. Bad memories, bad air."

Tommy nodded. "Yeah, I think you're right. It's like a monster was up there with us, and I'm not talking about you."

"You mean like a windigo?" Evan asked.

"I was talking about the lies, but yeah, there's definitely something creepy about this place."

He was pretty sure it was Albert he'd seen running through the woods when they were on the trail—the blue in his shirt was exactly the right shade. But what about the face he'd seen the woods? He'd been pretty frightened. He supposed it was possible that his imagination had made what he saw scarier than it really was.

He had to know for sure.

Chapter Fifteen

"Albert, were you following us when we were on the trail?"

Albert nodded. "I saw you, and then I ran up to the top. Needed to block the path so you wouldn't find me."

"You caused the first rock slide?"

"Uh-huh."

"But why the second slide? Didn't you want us to get off the mountain?"

"Didn't set the second slide. But when I started the first one, I guess I shook things up."

Tommy nodded. "Okay, so you were running in the woods. What about later? When our horses got scared, and mine took off into the woods...was that you I saw then too?" Remembering the hairy face and long yellow teeth he'd *thought* he'd seen made him shudder.

"Nope," Albert said. "After the second slide I was busy trying to clear a path for you. Pretty hard to do in secret when none of you was staying in the same place!"

"Oh," Tommy said. He peered into the woods. He saw tree-shaped shadows and wondered if that was what they really were. He tried not to think about how branches looked a lot like reaching arms.

He shuddered. If it wasn't Albert that he'd seen... what was it? He heard Colly sigh heavily, as if he was impatient.

"Colly," he said, "everyone else believes that there could be a bushman or a windigo in the woods. Why don't you?"

At first Colly looked annoyed, but then he sighed again. "It's not that I don't believe in spirits, it's just that I don't think we should be so quick to pin every mystery on them. I think if they want to show themselves, we won't have any question. I also *don't* think a bushman and the windigo spirit are the same thing. I don't know exactly what a bushman is, except that Albert isn't one of them. But a windigo...I don't think I ever want to find out."

Tommy considered this. Maybe it was best if he just didn't think about it too hard. Especially not here.

They walked for what felt like a very long time. Eventually, sweaty and thirsty, the raggle-taggle group rounded a bend and came in sight of Emerald Lake Ranch. Tommy was surprised to see not only the groups that had gone riding that morning, but also dozens of red-shirted Rangers, an ambulance and three Royal Canadian Mounted Police trucks.

Captain Conrad spotted them first, breaking into a run to meet them. The ambulance attendants and RCMP officers followed close behind. "Thank God!" he cried. "Some of the horses came back alone, so Jodi's ranch hands called us." He knelt beside Jodi, saw her eyes flutter open and called over the ambulance attendants. After they'd carried her to the ambulance on a stretcher, he turned to Jaz, who had slid to the ground, but was hopping on one foot.

"I thought my ankle was broken, but it feels a bit better now," she said. "It's probably just a bad sprain."

"Shelby, help Jaz over to the medics, will you?" he said. "Are the rest of you okay?" he asked.

"We're fine," Tommy said.

"What about your head?" Evan asked.

"Head?" Captain Conrad asked. He looked concerned.

"I'll get it checked later. First I want to introduce you to..." He turned and then stopped, confused. "Colly, did you see where Albert went?"

"No."

"Evan?"

"No, I was just so happy to see the ranch!"

Tommy scanned the woods, confused. Where had he gone?

"Who are you talking about, Tommy?" Captain Conrad asked.

"It's the guy Colly told us about at the campfire last night," Evan said.

"Refresh my memory."

"Albert Payne," Colly said. "Ten years ago his wife accused him of murdering her friend, and he disappeared into the woods. Turns out he was up on the Crank the whole time."

"Say that again?" one of the RCMP officers asked.

"Kids, this is Sergeant Dengle," Captain Conrad said. "He's been organizing your search team."

"Did I hear you say you were with Albert Payne?"

"Yes, sir," Tommy said, handing him the left-handed rifle. "This is proof that he's innocent."

Sergeant Dengle took the rifle and shook his head. "If it really was Payne you were with, you're lucky you got away. He's a dangerous man."

"But he was innocent," Evan said. "It was his wife who killed Bettyanne."

"His wife didn't kill anyone," he said. "She's been in a coma for twelve years."

Tommy glanced at Evan and Colly. They looked as stunned as he felt.

"His wife is in a coma?"

"That's right. We thought Payne was responsible for putting her there, but could never prove it. We think he killed his wife's friend when she confronted him about it. He disappeared before we could take him into custody."

Albert had said Jodi reminded him of his wife. It wasn't because of how she looked. It was because she was unconscious. "But...this is a left-handed rifle," Tommy said.

"Yes, and Payne was left-handed." Sergeant Dengle flipped the gun over and showed Tommy words engraved underneath. They read: *For my dear husband Albert, love Saphire.*

"It really is Albert's gun?" Tommy asked, eyes wide. "Not his wife's?"

"That's right."

Tommy gulped, trying to remember Albert doing something left- or right-handed. He couldn't really think of anything. He guessed he'd been too busy trying to think of a way out to notice a detail like that.

Something else confused him. "Albert must have known this gun would be evidence against him. Why would he give it to me and then just take off?"

Sergeant Dengle shrugged. "Who knows? Maybe he really was ready to turn himself in, but changed his mind at the last minute. Or maybe this is just his way of thumbing his nose at us. He was always like that."

"So, he was in trouble before Bettyanne died?" Colly asked.

"Yes. He got himself mixed up with some pretty nasty people in the year before he disappeared." Sergeant Dengle looked at each of them, his face deadly serious. "You are all very, very lucky. We're going to need to take a statement from each of you. But if you say he's in these woods, we're going after him right now. Any idea which way he went?"

They shook their heads. "No matter. This is closer than we've been in ten years." He pulled out his radio and began striding toward the RCMP trucks with his fellow officers.

"I'm glad you're all safe, especially considering the company you've been keeping," Captain Conrad said, shaking his head and rubbing his forehead. "Want to tell me the details?"

Tommy took a deep breath. "Yes, but I have something else I need to tell you first. Something about the fire at camp." He was surprised there were no nervous butterflies batting around in his belly, and relieved there were no creepy neck prickles.

He stole one last look at the wilderness they'd just come from. He didn't know for sure if he'd encountered a windigo in the woods, or whether it had been his own guilty conscious. Either way, he felt lucky to have survived. He felt strong.

What he'd said to Albert about lies making monsters was the truth. Albert was proof of that. He was one big monster. It didn't matter if Albert had chickened out, or if taking off was his plan all along. There was no way Tommy would let a lie, or anything else, mess him up like that.

Thinking of the face he'd seen, he shivered. It was possible that Albert was going to have to face something far worse in these woods than his lies.

He glanced at each of his friends. Shelby had returned and had her hand on his shoulder. Colly and Evan stood close.

"They're taking Jodi to the hospital," Shelby said. "But they think she's going to be okay."

Tommy glanced toward the ambulance where Jodi and Jaz were being treated. Jaz gave him a thumbs-up.

Captain Conrad was looking at him, frowning. "What about the fire, Tommy?"

Tommy hung his head. "The fire was an accident, Captain Conrad, but it was still my fault."

Captain Conrad frowned. He looked confused. "Go on," he said. "Tell me what happened."

Tommy felt something leave him then, some swirling dark thing that he couldn't explain, and he smiled. The situation was serious, but Tommy couldn't help smiling. He always smiled. He was the type of person who smiled because it was sunny or because he was out in his boat. Everyone knew that about him.

This time his smile meant that, no matter what happened next, everything was going to be okay.

Acknowledgments

Deepest thanks to my editor Sarah Harvey, whose skill, as always, blew me away as she helped me find the true shape of this story; to my sister Heather, at whose kitchen table the JCR stories were birthed; to my family—Jim for his tolerance, Sara for reading over the horse bits and sharing her horse and taking author photos, and Erin for letting Sara use her camera; to Richard Van Camp for friendship and many discussions about bushmen and the windigo spirit; to Captain Conrad Schubert for his continuing support and his keen eye as first reader; to my agent Marie Campbell for encouragement and so much more; to Bernie and Pam Phillips from Historical House B & B for a terrific stay and for not telling me about the ghost until I was leaving; to Joni MacKinnon from the real Emerald Lake Ranch for sharing her horses, trails and the magic of the mountains she calls home; to Tracey Anderson from the MacBride Museum for Yukon stories, history and floor plans; to the Manitoba Arts Council for financial support during my research trip; to Kelly Hughes and all the staff of Aqua Books who encouraged me daily to write and eat cheesecake; to Debbie Webster for her help with Tommy Toner's name and her thoughts about how cultural identity can be determined by factors other than blood.

Once again, I have taken one or two real names and pasted them on characters. I've done this out of respect, and because I think their names are peachy keen.

No real horse wranglers were injured in the making of this story.

Anita Daher's writing reflects the places she's been blessed to spend time. Earlier Orca thrillers for young readers are *Flight from Big Tangle*, *Flight from Bear Canyon*, *Racing for Diamonds* and *Poachers in the Pingos*. She has also written *Two Foot Punch*, a sports thriller about free running. Anita lives in Manitoba, dividing her time between Winnipeg and the Francophone community of St. Georges, where she walks by the river and is learning how to read the signs. Find out more about Anita and her books on her website at www.anitadaher.com.